Tots and the
Snowy Blowy Day

Written by Ragdoll

Illustrated by Penny Lane

A Ragdoll Production for Central Independent Television

Scholastic Children's Books,
7-9 Pratt Street, London NW1 0AE UK
A division of Scholastic Publications Ltd
London—New York—Toronto—Sydney—Auckland

Published by Scholastic Publications Ltd, 1995

Text copyright © Ragdoll Productions (UK) Ltd 1995
Illustrations copyright © Penny Lane 1995
Text by Jack Ousbey

Design of Tots TV puppets and house copyright
© Ragdoll Productions (UK) Ltd 1993
Central logo copyright © Central Independent TV plc 1989
Based on the Central Independent Television series produced by Ragdoll Productions

ISBN 0 590 55794 7

Typeset by Rapid Repographics
Printed in Great Britain by Bath Press Colourbooks, Glasgow

10 9 8 7 6 5 4 3 2

The right of Jack Ousbey and Penny Lane to be identified as the author and
illustrator of this work has been asserted by them in accordance with the
Copyright, Designs and Patents Act, 1988.

All was quiet in the secret house where the Tots lived. Tilly woke up first.

"Bonjour, Tots," she said.

"Good morning, Tilly," said Tiny.

"Tots," said Tom, "I think something interesting is going to happen today. I have a feeling, I have."

Tiny took the magic bag from its peg and they were ready to go adventuring out.

"Eee-aw," said Donkey as they went through the garden.

"What will we see today?" sang the Tots. "What will we see?"

"Peek-a-boo," said Furryboo.

Tilly, Tom and Tiny had been waiting for it to snow for many days. Tom was getting his sledge ready, and Tilly had knitted a red hat, and a blue and green scarf for the snowman she planned to make.

"I wish it would snow," said Tom.
"I wish it would snow," said Tiny.
"Attendez," said Tilly. "Un moment."

When Tilly came back, she was carrying something very carefully.

"Red boots," said Tiny. "A little pair of beautiful red boots."

9

"Mmm," said Tom. "A particularly nice pair of boots those are, but what are we going to do with them?"

"Regardez," said Tilly as she pulled on the boots. "Je suis danseuse," and she began to dance. As she tipped and tapped, this way and that, she played a little tune on her flute.

Tom put some words to the tune and he and Tiny sang:

The Red Boot toes go tip-tip-tip;
The Red Boot heels go tap-tap-tap;
Heels and toes go step-step-step;
Red Boots dancing, clap-clap-clap.

"Les bottillons – ils sont magiques," said Tilly, catching her breath.

"What do you mean, Tilly," said Tom. "How are they magic?"

"Maybe they could magic some snow for us," said Tiny. "That's the kind of magic we really need."

"Ecoutez," said Tilly, and she began to play again.

Very quickly, very softly they sang a special, magic, snow-spell song which they had just made up.

Tom and Tiny sang:

Moon in the sky, yellow and round,
Send thousands of snowflakes to
cover the ground;
Frosty old stars make never a sound,
Just send thousands of snowflakes to
cover the ground.
Thousands of snowflakes, thousands of snowflakes,
Thousands of snowflakes to cover the ground.

The Tots waited. Tilly continued to play her flute softly, and at last, a thick, soft snow flake settled on the window, and then another and another.

"Hourra," said Tilly. "Il neige."

"Yippee," shouted Tiny. "It's snowing."

"It's blowing and snowing and covering the ground," said Tom.

Tiny set off at full speed, through the door and out into the snow with a great leap. Tilly ran after him in her woolly hat and magic red boots. Tom followed with his sledge.

17

When no one was looking, Furryboo slipped out to see what was causing all the excitement.

"This way for Tom's amazing sledge ride," called Tom. Tilly had a ride first, all the way round the house, pulled by Tom and Tiny.

Then they decided to help Tilly make her snowman.

They rolled a ball of snow round and round and round the garden, singing and chanting as they worked, then tipped it on to its side to make the body. It was now so big, they had to make snow steps so that Tilly could reach up to put the head on. Then she found him snowman buttons and a carrot nose.

Tilly's snowman was almost finished. He was wearing his red hat and his blue and green scarf. She asked Tom and Tiny what they thought about him.

"He's a very nice old snowman," said Tom, "but he looks lonely."

"Yes," said Tiny. "He does look a bit lonely, actually, standing there on his own."

And he and Tom began to chant:

That snowman is lonely out there on his own,
Out there on his own, out there on his own.
That snowman is lonely out there on his own,
So we'll build him some snow Tots for company.

24

"Une bonne idée," said Tilly. "Un Tom, un Tiny et une Tilly."

At first, the little snow Tots didn't look too much like Tiny, Tilly and Tom, until they found some coloured wool and made red, green and blue hair.

This one is Tiny, this one is Tom,
This one is Tilly with dancing boots on.
The snowman looks happy and seems to agree
It's nice having snow Tots for company.

Later, before they went up to bed, they made up a
new, goodnight song. As they went upstairs, they
heard Donkey "Eee-aw" from outside. When they
were ready for bed they stood, hand in hand, in front
of the window and looked out on the garden.

Through the swirling snowflakes they could see the figures of the snowman and the snow Tots. They seemed to be looking up at the bedroom window.

Very softly and very quietly, Tilly, Tom and Tiny
sang their special goodnight song:

The snowy blowy day is over,
The snowy blowy day is done.
We've had lots of snowy blowy adventures
And quite a lot of snowy blowy fun.
Now it's snowy blowy time for sleeping
In beds that are snowy blowy white,
And snowy blowy dreams are creeping
At the end of this snowy blowy night.

"We've had the most magical, dancey prancey, snowy blowy day," whispered Tiny. He was almost asleep before he had finished saying it.

   "Mmmm," said Tilly.
   "Ahhh," said Tom.

And from somewhere in the rafters, Furryboo gave a little peek-a-boo.